# Driving Down The Hollywood Boulevard

Pavitr Tomar

INDIA • SINGAPORE • MALAYSIA

**1**

Ahlam is a 25-year-old boy of Indian origin who lives in Downtown, Los Angeles. He hails from Bombay, the capital of Bollywood, the biggest piece of the Indian cinema pie. Ahlam was born into a very conservative Indian family, where dreaming big is not allowed. After completing his bachelor's degree in India, Ahlam decided to pursue his master's degree in journalism in the United States of America. He saved up enough money to fund his education in America so that he could live his American dream.

What was Ahlam's American dream? To find a lucrative 9-to-5 job or to live a comfortable life with a beautiful wife and enchanting children? It wasn't either of those. He wanted to become a well-established actor in Hollywood. For Ahlam, pursuing his master's in America was just an escape gate to evade the morbid reality that had penetrated its roots deep into typical Indian societies.

In India, as soon as a boy is born, he is directed to study hard and find himself a job that will make his and his parents' lives milk and honey. And then he has to marry a girl that he has never met even once, make beautiful children with her, and then grace himself with a peaceful death with grandchildren around. That is what they call 'The Circle of Life'.

Ahlam was not looking forward to falling into this trap. All he excogitated for himself was a dream away from the Stereotypical thinking of his peers, and when he made up his mind to transform his dream into a reality, there was no looking back.

W hen Ahlam was 15 years old, his *abba* Tahir introduced him to cricket. He used to train Ahlam for hours, so, he could become the next Zaheer Khan. But Ahlam was not interested in cricket. All he wanted to do was sprint back home and imitate his favourite scenes from his favourite movies. Whenever his abba used to throw a ball towards him, his delicate hands used to tremble, missing the ball by several inches. One day his abba got infuriated and vented.

'I am wearied by your persistent fragility. Ahlam! Your delicate hands can't even hold the bat properly, and I expect you to be a cricketer.› Abba said.

'I am sorry, abba,' Ahlam said, trembling.

'I would rather have been blessed with a girl than a son like you. After all, what's the difference between you and a girl?'

Ahlam's head drooped with a gloomy expression on his face.

These words by his abba left Ahlam's heart shattered. He threw his bat away, smashed his helmet several times on the concrete, and started crying his heart out.

His abba meant the world to Ahlam. When Ahlam was young, his Abba used to carry him on his back, and they used to stroll to the local fair, savouring everything Ahlam pointed his finger at. Ahlam's abba was fond of birdwatching, so he used to take him to the nearby parks, and they used to lie down on their backs and spend their whole day watching countless birds. Ahlam used to crouch behind the trees in the park and watch the squirrels hiding their nuts in the ground. Ahlam and his abba shared an inseparable bond. But slowly, that bond dwindled because of Ahlam's effeminacy.

Ahlam had effeminate traits. He was fond of girls' clothing, so he used to dress up in his mother's attire and used to wander around the house crooning Bollywood songs, imitating the expressions and dance moves, disguising himself as an actress. His abba used to find his behaviour distasteful. One day, he came home from work and saw him dancing in his mother's clothes. He sprinted towards him and started snatching his clothes, tearing them apart, and leaving him naked. Ahlam's mother rushed towards him and covered him with her scarf.

It wasn't just his abba, who found his behaviour distasteful but his classmates and friends too. Ahlam was ridiculed by most of his classmates. They used to call him by several names, like loser, gay, girlish boy, etc. For

Ahlam, bullying was not only restricted to being called names, he was also physically harmed several times. A bullying episode during his 11th-grade convocation day turned into the nightmare of a lifetime. Ahlam was walking home from school when two boys jumped out of nowhere, pushed him into the junkyard, and started whacking him with an iron object. He screamed for help, but his screams went unheard. After two hours, he noticed chunks of hair being pulled out of his head. There were bruises all over his body. His jaw was sprained. He picked himself up, reached home, went straight to his washroom, turned the faucet into the bucket so nobody could hear him, and cried his heart out.

He faced all sorts of bullying just because he was an effeminate, introvert and always asked for acceptance. The Acceptance never came from his friends or his abba.

The only person who accepted Ahlam's effeminacy was his *ammi,* because she believed Ahlam was born this way and nobody could ever change him or his behaviour. She loved him selflessly. As soon as Ahlam came home from school, his ammi always used to cook his favourite urad-dal with rice and, after eating his favourite meal. He used to forget everything that happened in school. A nap during the midday hours was his best time of the day because it was the only portal to his dream world. He used to rest his head on his mother's nurturing lap and doze off for an hour or two.

He used to dream the same thing every day, picking his attire for the Oscars: a black tuxedo with a white shirt, black shoes, a miniature bow tie, and goofy socks. His hair combed to the right side, and a smiling face, just like the Joker. A walk down the red carpet, surrounded by the paparazzi, sitting in the front row with Matthew McConaughey sitting next to him, giggling, chatting, and waiting restlessly for the Academy Award for Best Actor in a Leading Role category. Then comes the moment Ahlam used to wait eagerly, the time to announce the winner of the category he's nominated in. Amy Adams comes up on stage as the announcer, and her sweet voice goes, 'Academy Award for Best Actor in a Leading Role goes to Ahlam Siddique! Ahlam bounces out of his chair in excitement, hugs Matthew McConaughey, and walks up to the stage, wiping his tears as commentators brief, in the background.

*It is Ahlam Siddique's first Academy Award and as well as his first nomination. He is the first Indian actor to ever win an Academy Award.*

Amy Adams hands the Oscar to Ahlam and he stands in front of thousands of people and gives his Oscar speech.

**3**

There must be an alternative universe that exists where Ahlam is a film star, like the universe in Everything Everywhere All at Once, where Evelyn is an actress, not any bourgeois woman who owns a small business and is wearied with her life. Ahlam believed his dreams were the only portal to the exquisite and luxurious life where he is surrounded by people who adore him, and he wanted his life in the prevailing universe to be just like his life in the alternative universe, but his imaginary life was far away from the morbid reality he was living in. Instead of being surrounded by encouraging people, he was surrounded by people who would feed off his talent and art just like parasites. Ahlam was determined to convert his dream into reality, and he knew that his life was filled with intruders who would always poke their noses in his business, but he was stubborn and he would never let go of his passion.

Fifteen years ago, Ahlam was willing to pursue the life his parents premeditated for him, but what flashed into Ahlam's mind that made him follow his world of fantasies instead of the life his parents chose for him?

When Ahlam was fifteen years old, his parents welcomed a new device called a television into their home. A small screen with many vibrant colours and figures moving around started to fascinate him.

When his parents used to go to work, he used to switch on the television and dance gayly to Bollywood songs.

One day his friend Rahim brought a CD home consisting of numerous English movies, and out of all the movies, they decided to watch Monster, a 2003 film starring Charlize Theron. It was only when he got introduced to real cinema and learned what authentic acting is. Charlize Theron's Oscar-winning performance left him so flabbergasted that he decided he wanted to become an actor and work in the cinema.

Every day he used to watch a new movie and imitate its scenes, and this continued for months until one day, Ahlam got all courageous and confronted his abba.

'Abba, I have tried to pursue the dream you saw for me, but I failed miserably, I know I have disappointed you, and I am sorry.› Ahlam said.

'Decipher what you're saying.' Abba said, placing his newspaper down and lowering his glasses.

'All I ever wanted to be was an actor, I have lived that dream for so long but never gathered the courage to tell you.'

Ahlam's abba looked at him with his eyes wide open, and without saying a word, he gave a tight slap to Ahlam's face. Ahlam got infuriated and ran out of his home, weeping heavily, and sat on a bench at the nearby park and screamed as loud as he could. He stayed there for hours and didn't return home that day. When he returned home at dawn, he saw his house ransacked.

'What happened, Ammi?› Ahlam yelled.

'Ahlam, I told you to never tell your abba about your dream.› Ammi said this while sobbing.

'But I thought he would understand what his child wants, and I can't suffocate myself anymore, Ammi.'

'He will never understand Ahlam, Leave this house before your abba returns and stay at Zainab's residence for some days.'

Ahlam picked out some clothes from his cupboard, wrapped them in his ammi's scarf, and left the house. Zainab was Ahlam's ammi's school friend, and he loathed her and always avoided visiting her because she used to maltreat him. But there was no other residence left for him where he could reside, so he reached Zainab's house, and as soon as he rang the bell, Zainab opened the door with a crease on her forehead.

'Kids like you are born to disappoint their parents.'

Ahlam listened quietly and didn't utter anything.

'Say what you want to say, I know you have a lot of garbage in your mind.'

'Nothing; ammi told me to Stay at your residence for some days but you know what, I would rather sleep on a park bench than sleep on your filthy bed.'

'Then get out, and never show me this disappointing face again.'

Ahlam lifted his pile of clothes and went as far as he could from Zainab's house.

**4**

While walking, he saw a small theatre with a bunch of movies on air and he thought of converting the adversity into an opportunity, he walked into the theatre and stood near the ticket counter until the ticket clerk called him and asked,

'You have been standing here for ten minutes now, what do you want?'

'A job,› Ahlam said hesitantly.

'How old are you?'

'Eighteen.'

'We are already full-on employees, but you can work as an unpaid intern if you want.'

'But I don't have any place to live and no food to eat; can you give me a small amount of money so I can have my necessities?'

'I can only buy you lunch and allow you to sleep inside the theatre at night, that's everything I can do.'

'That would be enough, thank you.› Ahlam said with shiny eyes.

Ahlam starts walking towards the exit, and the ticket clerk shouts.

'Where are you going?'

'Nowhere, just going to take a stroll outside.› Ahlam said.

'But you have a shift.'

'When?'

'Now,'

'Now?'

'Yes, go stand inside theatre number two and inform me as soon as any inconvenience occurs during the showtime.'

Ahlam Stood inside the theatre and the theatre started filling up with people. A movie flashed on the screen, titled 'The Departed' and Ahlam couldn't take his eyes off the screen for two and a half hours because he became so lost in Jack Nicholson's magnificent acting and the movie's dynamic plot, that he forgot to inform the ticket clerk that light didn't go off during the whole screentime. Ahlam timidly walked out of the theatre and saw the ticket clerk Standing vexed and holding the feedback box containing several complaints.

'This is how you're going to work every day?'

'I am sorry, I forgot to tell you about the lights.'

'This is your last chance, next time if I see any negative feedback in the feedback box, I will kick you out.'

'Okay, I will take care of it.'

## 5

Ahlam loved his job; all he had to do was watch movies all day and inform the ticket clerk in case any inconvenience occurred in the theatre. He worked in the theatre for a month and saw an abundance of intriguing movies, which increased his desire to be a movie star. He saw The Holiday and liked the concept of people exchanging their lives with each other, and he wished he could change his life with a prominent actor. Little Miss Sunshine stole his heart; Olive didn't give up on her dream to participate in a beauty pageant; and her family didn't refrain from accompanying her on the journey. The Pursuit of Happiness taught him that you must keep working hard until your good time comes. The Black Dahlia made him cry as he saw a girl's dream broken into a million tiny pieces. Helen Mirren's acting in The Queen introduced him to versatility. Meryl Streep's role in The Devil Wears the Prada made him realise that negative characters in movies could still make an impact and bring you an overwhelming feeling. The Last King of Scotland turned out to be the best movie he ever saw, from Forest Whitaker's performance of a lifetime to the direction of the movie, everything won his heart. He found a lost part of his childhood in Happy Feet, but Pan's Labyrinth scared him for days. Borat made him laugh uncontrollably, and United 93 made him cry his heart out. The Departed made him sit on the edge of his seat, and Little Children made him peek through the space between his fingers as he felt shy watching the erotic scenes.

He learned countless things from all the movies he saw while working in the theatre, which made him more determined to be an actor.

6

Ahlam was living his best life until one day theatre cleaner Rustam approached Ahlam.

'Your abba's calling you, Ahlam.› Rustum said, hysterically.

'I don't like this kind of prank, Rustam.' Ahlam said.

'I am not pranking you, your abba's really standing outside the theatre.'

Ahlam's skin turned pale, and he ran as fast as he could to corroborate if his abba was really standing outside.

'Abba?' Ahlam said.

'Come back home *beta*, it's been three months since you left your home.' Abba said, teary-eyed.

'But abba I never expected you to come here, I thought I let you down, and you never want to see my face again'

'A father could never see his child homeless and wandering on the streets.'

'How did you find me, abba?'

'The ticket clerk that gave you the job is my friend, and when he saw you approaching him, he gave me a call, and I appealed to him to give you a job.'

'Why, abba, if you find me so distasteful, why do you want to help me?'

'Because I love you, Ahlam, I may never show it but a piece of my heart belongs to you, and the whole house looks empty without you.'

Hearing his abba's words, Ahlam burst into tears, and he ran and hugged his abba tightly.

'I love you too, abba. I know I have been a bad child, but I will try to improve myself.'

'There are no bad people, Ahlam, just bad situations, and we have to cope with them.'

Ahlam held his abba's hand, and they headed towards their home. As soon as Ahlam entered the house, his mother overwhelmingly shouted in happiness and held him in her arms. At last, the adversity ended, and they all ate their dinner together and headed to sleep.

**7**

Ahlam was back to living his comfortable life in his snuggly home, but he wasn't as content as he was when he used to work in the theatre. He was missing the theatre and wanted to visit there again, but suddenly his memory was evoked, and he recalled that he has a television and it could work as an alternative to the theatre. He went straight to the living room, but the television wasn't there. He confronted his mother.

'Ammi, where is the television?' Ahlam said.

'Your abba broke it in rage.' Ammi said.

'How will I watch movies now?'

'Why do you want to watch movies anyway, focus on your Studies Ahlam, your exams are coming up.'

'Ammi, I am studying for 2-3 hours at night, what else do you want me to do? Watching movies is the only thing that relaxes me.'

'We have the DVD player intact, you can use it.'

'Ammi, a DVD player is of no use without the television.'

'Study hard, get a job, and buy yourself a new television.'

Ahlam disregarded what her mother was saying. He picked up the DVD player and went straight to Rahim's house. He connected the DVD player to Rahim's television, and their conversation turned into a brawl. Ahlam wanted to watch The Shawshank Redemption, but Rahim wanted to watch Spider-Man 3. After a long fight, they both agreed to watch a movie that created the Oscar buzz back in 1998. They both sat on the couch. Ahlam placed the CD inside the DVD player, and a movie titled 'American Beauty' appeared on the screen. The movie seemed interesting and quite simple at first glance, but soon it took a turn of events in its plot, with Angela Hayes lying on a bed of roses, smiling, and wearing absolutely nothing. They couldn't take their eyes off her. Their brain was telling them to turn off the television, but their hearts were telling them to keep watching, so as amateur kids who had just stepped into adulthood, they listened to their hearts. Their eyes turned red and dry, but blinking seemed like an impossible task to them. They just kept gazing. They were so lost in the movie that they didn't even hear that someone was constantly knocking on the door. A loud voice went through their ears.

'Rahim, open the door!' Rahim's abba shouted.

'It's abba, we have to turn off the television now.' Rahim said.

'Do you want to?' Ahlam said.

'No, I don't want to but I have to.'

Rahim stood up and turned the television off.

'What are you watching, kids?'

'American B…'

'American Graffiti, abba.'

'Oh, that 1973 movie?'

'Yes, abba.'

'I would like to watch it too; let's all watch it together.'

'Abba, we have already watched it past the interval.'

'Oh, come on, watch it again with me.'

Before Rahim could make another excuse, his abba walked towards the television, turned it on, and kept glaring at the screen for a minute.

'It doesn't look like American Graffiti to me.'

'It is American Graffiti abba, maybe you watched it a long time ago, so you don't remember this scene.'

'I have watched American Graffiti three times, how could I not remember this scene?'

Rahim's abba glanced at the cover lying beside the DVD player and read the title as loud as he could.

'American Beauty?'

'It was Ahlam's plan, abba; he wanted to watch this movie, but I didn't, I warned him several times that this movie contained erotic scenes, but he didn't listen to me.' Rahim said to defend himself.

'Stop lying, Rahim!'

Rahim's abba looked at Ahlam and strode towards him.

'Go home, I'll come and meet your abba today.'

'I am sorry, uncle, we won't do it again.'

Rahim's abba ignored Ahlam's apology. Ahlam walked out of Rahim's house and advanced towards his house. Ahlam knew Rahim's abba would come to his house and confront his abba and his abba would reprimand him. With his heart beating faster than ever, he covered himself with his blanket and tried to doze off. As he was about to fall asleep, he heard the main door getting banged into the wall, and he heard a loud voice.

'Tahir, where are you?' said Rahim's abba.

'He's at work, bhaiya.' said Ahlam's ammi.

'Tell him to visit me as soon as he comes home.'

'What happened?'

'What a shameless son you have.'

'Mind your language, bhaiya, what did he even do?'

'Your nasty son made my son watch a very dirty movie.'

' He could never do such a thing.'

'He did, They both were watching American Beauty.'

'Did you say 'both'?'

'Yes, both!'

'If both were watching, then both are equally responsible for their actions, and both should face the consequences. So, instead of blaming Ahlam for everything, try reprimanding Rahim.'

'But Rahim told me it was your son who forced him into watching this kind of movie.'

'But you said both were watching the movie together, so they both agreed on watching it together, and if Rahim didn't want to watch the movie, he could have simply denied it and walked away, but he didn't, he kept watching until you caught both of them.'

'But…'

'You have said enough, I can't stand you contradicting your statements, The exit is right behind you!'

Rahim's abba left the house, mumbling to himself. Ahlam came out of his room, and his ammi gave him a death stare.

'Rahim's abba told me something about you.' Ammi said.

'I have heard everything, ammi, I'll never do such a thing again.› Ahlam said.

'If you want to see your ammi happy and thriving, stop watching movies.'

'I can't, movies are something I live for, this is my passion, ammi.'

'I know Ahlam, but do it for your ammi, Every brawl that happens in this house is because of this passion of yours, bury your passion for sometimes and do what makes your abba happy.'

'What if I don't want to bury it?'

'Then one day this small family of ours will fall apart.'

These words hit Ahlam like lightning. He sat on the couch just behind him and started to rethink his life decisions. He had a choice to make.

## 8

Ahlam had a choice to make whether manifest his parents' dream or manifest his own dream.

The big Hollywood dream that he constructed for himself wasn't a cup of tea, he knew that he has to work hard and suffer a lot to transform his dream into a reality, and if he would be successful in doing such, it would bring him immense satisfaction and he could live his life with no regrets. On the other hand, his parents wanted him to get succumbed into their so-called 'The Circle of Life' thing and he knew if he fell into this never-ending circle, he would never come out of it. It's like a black hole for an average Indian kid, where you could fall inside it but never make it outside. A 9-to-5 job where he only has to sit on a counter with a lousy face and just bang his fingers on the keyboards continuously until his boss tells him to stop. It was more of a nightmare for him than a wholesome dream. Marrying a girl and having children with her who would keep screaming in his ears all day long and then watching them grow up and sitting by his side on his deathbed wasn't something he wanted to buy.

But if he chose to manifest the big Hollywood dream, he knew he would lose his ammi and abbu. The fear of losing his parents made Ahlam choose the life his parents premeditated for him.

Ahlam's ammi was mopping the floor, and he called her.

'Ammi, I want to tell you something!'

'We'll talk later, I have so much work left to do.'

'Ammi, the news I'm about to tell you will bring you the happiness of your lifetime, you have to listen to this!'

'say,'

' I want to be an article writer just like abba.'

'Have I gone deaf? or are you really saying this?'

'Yes ammi, I am ready to pursue the dream that you and abbu saw for me.'

'Ahlam, you have no idea how elated your abba will be after hearing this news.'

'I know, ammi, I don't want to see our family fall apart.'

Ahlam's ammi hugged him tightly and sprinted to call her husband on the telephone. Ahlam felt lighthearted after a long time, knowing he did the right thing.

**9**

Ahlam felt delighted to see her mother ecstatic, but there was something else going on inside his head. Everything he said was part of a plan that he came up with.

If his parents condemned movies so much and didn't want Ahlam to think about them at all, then why shouldn't he make his parents hear something that will feel pleasurable to their ears? It will make Ahlam and his parents feel happy-go-lucky. As soon as Ahlam's husky voice went through his parents' ears, saying, 'I want to be an article writer just like abba', his parents started flying in the air with invisible wings while weeping at the same time. His abba made abundant promises to him, and Ahlam just kept listening to his fake covenants.

'I will provide you the kind of education that nobody in this city ever provided to their child,' Abba said.

'What kind of education?' Ahlam said.

'The finest, I will send you to the best college in the city.'

'Abba can I study at St. Xavier's College? It provides the best education among all the colleges in the city.'

'Then, I'll definitely send you there.'

St. Xavier's was famous not only for its education but also for its connection to Bollywood. If you would google St. Xavier's College, you would find the finest actors in Bollywood as its alumni. Ahlam knew that getting into this college would bring him one step closer to becoming an actor.

Ahlam was growing deceitful towards his parents, and he could've done anything to get closer to his dream life.

Ahlam studied day and night and gave his 12th-grade board examination.

'When is your result coming, Ahlam?› Ammi said.

'Anytime now!' Ahlam said.

'Are you scared?'

'Not at all, I know I'd score good marks.'

'I know you studied all day and night, and hard work pays off.'

'Results are out, ammi.'

'When?'

'Just now!'

'How much did you score?'

'A whopping ninety-two percent.'

'Oh, my sweet Ahlam, I knew you would make your parents proud.'

Ammi kissed Ahlam on the forehead and went inside the kitchen to make Ahlam's favourite rasmalai. Ahlam was jumping up and down with contentment, knowing that he would make it to the cut-off and would get into St. Xavier's College, and his dream of becoming an actor could become a reality. He started thinking of all the plays and dramas he could be a part of at St. Xavier's and how much exposure he would get there.

Acting for the first time on a stage in front of hundreds of people would be a thrilling experience for him.

The next hour, Ahlam and his abba went to St. Xavier's and filled out the Bachelor in Mass Media registration form. He went shopping with her mother, bought new clothes and a brand-new mobile phone, and packed up his bags. The response came on July 28 through email, saying,

*Dear Ahlam Siddique,*

*Congratulations on qualifying in your admission rounds and earning an offer of admission to the Bachelor in Mass Media programme at St. Xavier's Autonomous College.*

*We request that you refer to the attached letter for details of your offer. You are required to send us the completed acceptance note and the registration fee receipt before the deadline, which is August 28, 2006.*

*For any queries, please contact the undersigned.*

*Regards,*
*— **Ajay Anand***
*Assistant Manager,*
*Admissions & Outreach*
*St Xavier's Autonomous College*

Ahlam felt intrigued, seeing the email, and he sprinted towards his abbas's office.

'Abba, I got in!' Ahlam shouted in excitement.

'Where?' Abba said.

'In St. Xavier's.'

'I'm so proud of you, Ahlam.

'Thank You, abba,'

'When will we be leaving for college?'

'Tomorrow.'

'Tomorrow? Isn't it too early?'

'The earlier you leave, the more you'll learn!'

'Okay, abba.'

The next day, Ahlam picked up his bags and left for college with his abba. Ahlam was thrilled, and it was visible on his face. On the other side, abba's expression was telling that he was very proud of Ahlam. They reached the college, paid the fees, and headed towards Ahlam's hostel room. As soon as they entered the room, they saw three boys sitting on their respective beds. Ahlam held his abba's wrist, indicating him to step out of the room with him. They stepped out and closed the door.

'Abba, I can't live with three strangers.' Ahlam said.

'Should I buy you a private apartment, so you could live a comfortable life in solitude, your majesty,' Abba said.

'Abba I am not kidding, can we please look for a room where I could live alone?'

'We can't afford that, Ahlam; you have to share your room with other people.'

'Abba, It's like a nightmare for me to share my room with other people, I am an introvert.'

'Sometimes you have to come out of your shell, Ahlam, everything can't be arranged according to your convenience.'

'But abba…'

'There's no if and but, live with these people or travel twenty-five kilometres every day, attend college, and come back home.'

'I can't travel twenty-five kilometres every day.'

'Then live the best time of your life here, When I was your age, I enjoyed my hostel life to the fullest, and you should too.'

'Alright abba, I'll try,'

Abba left the hostel, and Ahlam was left alone with strangers. Ahlam wanted to enter the room and introduce himself to his roommates, but his introverted personality was preventing him from doing so. His legs were shaking, but he slowly started sliding his right foot forward. He opened the door and saw three expressionless faces.

'Hi, I am Ahlam' Ahlam said.

'You will sleep on the floor, there's no bed available for you.' Rohan, Ahlam's roommate said.

'Why?'

'Because I'm telling you to.'

'But one bed is not occupied by anybody.'

'Which one?'

'The one next to yours.'

'That's also mine, I will stack my clothes up there.'

'Can I at least have a mattress?'

'You can have a bedsheet.'

'What would I do with a bedsheet if you won't let me have a bed?'

'Spread it on the floor and sleep on it.'

Ahlam stacked up his luggage in the corner and left the room.

*What do these people think of themselves? I was so joyous about going to college and meeting new people, but these people are monsters, and I hate them.*

Tears started rolling out of his eyes, but he kept on mumbling.

*Not only these people are monsters, but everybody I ever met is a monster. These people are filthy scavengers who only know how to feed off people who are dead inside. I wish God would have built a world for people like me, where we could live our lives peacefully without all these filthy people around, where I would thrive and do everything I ever wanted to do without any hindrance, but I am here living in a world created by God but ruled by monsters.*

Ahlam was sitting on the stairs in the middle of the hallway, and everybody passing by was looking at him, sobbing like a child.

*Now these people would look at me and laugh at me. Crying is like a sin for boys. Abba used to tell me, 'Boys don't cry› .I will cry whenever I want to and how could I expect these emotionless people to understand my emotions?*

*I am a mess, sitting between 6.6 billion worth of mess, and the mess keeps on increasing every day, every hour, every minute, and every second.*

Ahlam gathered all his courage, stood up, and reminded himself.

*Now I will tell these people their worth, my abba paid for a bed, so why can't I use it? Who are these people to tell me that I can't use the bed assigned to me?*

Ahlam stood outside the hostel room and banged his fist on the door as loud as he could. His roommate, Rohan, opened the door.

'What do you want?' Rohan said.

'I just wanted to tell you that I'm not going to sleep on the floor.' Ahlam said.

'You have to.'

'No, I don't have to, I paid for a bed, and I will sleep on it.'

'Don't you understand English?'

'I do, and in the English language, I'm telling you to remove your stuff from my bed.'

'Akshya, come here for a second, this boy needs to learn a lesson.'

'What should we do with him?' Akshya said.

'If you even try to touch me, I will write a letter to the college administration and the nearest police station, and you will be thrown out of the college and will end up in jail for about five years.'

'Are you threatening us?'

'No, I am just humbly informing you of the consequences of bullying someone.'

Rohan cracked his knuckles and punched Ahlam on the nose. Ahlam blacked out and fell to the floor.

**11**

Ahlam woke up after several hours and found himself locked in a washroom. The washroom was pitch black. He picked himself up and shouted.

'Is anyone there?'

*No answer.*

'Please open the door, I am scared of darkness.'

No Answers Again. Ahlam felt his heart palpitating. He kept looking around the dark room, praying and whispering the verses from *the Quran* while he was swinging himself back and forth, and soon he heard a loud bang on the door.

'Who is it?' Ahlam said.

'Your nightmare!' Rohan said.

'Please get me out of here.'

'No, you wanted a place to sleep, we were condoling enough to give you one, but your greed didn't suffice, so this is the place where you would be sleeping for the next twenty-four hours.'

'I can't sleep in here, I have *phasmophobia*'

'What is *phasmophobia*? '

'Fear of ghosts.'

'Now, it's time for you to bid goodbye to your phobia, Good Night.'

Ahlam closed his eyes and didn't stop praying for a second. It's been five hours since he's been praying, and he apprehended something.

*I have been sitting in this washroom for five hours now, but I haven't seen a glance of a ghost, all I could see is darkness, which is soothing and peaceful, and there's nobody around to bully or reprimand me. Just me and the darkness.*

Ahlam started to think of all the movie scenes he had imitated before, and he started re-imitating them because Ahlam believed he was his biggest critic, and when he wouldn't be able to see himself in the mirror while imitating, he wouldn't criticise his expressions. He imitated scenes from Gladiator, Gone with the Wind, A Beautiful Mind, etc and he found immense pleasure in enacting scenes without any criticism.

It had been thirteen hours since he'd been locked in the washroom, and he had done everything that he could inside that 40 by 100-square-foot room. A chain of thoughts started flickering inside his mind.

*Why did I decide to be an actor in the first place? I could have dreamt of anything that could have made ammi and abbu happy, but, why did I dream of something that would bring nothing but misery to my family? It might be because I was good at something and I wanted to fill an empty void. Everyone was good at something. Rahul was good at playing tennis, Sheena loved dancing, and Ahmed wanted to be a cricketer, but whenever I tried to discover if I was good at something, I found only flaws instead of qualities. But when Rahim made me watch Monster (2003), I felt something in a certain way. I felt an urge to imitate Charlize Theron's expressions, her way of venting and delivering dialogue, and when Rahim left my home, I tried enacting Aileen Wuornos from Monster, and I found out this is something I'm good at and this is what I want to become, 'An actor.' That day I started to dream about the beautiful yet hardworking life of Hollywood, and I couldn't look back even if I tried.*

*I thought of transforming my dream into reality, and I always worked hard for it, but eventually, I am stuck here, inside this dirty, pitch-black washroom, They say when life gives you lemons, make lemonade, but my life gave me lemons that were rotten from inside, you either drink the insipid lemonade or you don't drink it at all.*

While Ahlam was lost in his never-ending chain of thoughts, Akshya opened the door as he wanted to use the washroom urgently.

'Hey, get out of the washroom for a minute.' Akshya said.

'Why?' Ahlam said.

'I want to pee.'

'If I get out, your boss will beat the hell out of me.'

'He isn't here.'

'Okay, I'm going out.'

Ahlam gets up and begins to walk out of the washroom.

'Don't run away.'

'I won't.'

'You don't know the consequences of refraining from Rohan's orders, He is the son of a prominent minister, and no one in this college has the audacity to get in a brawl with him.'

'So, you're going to lock me inside again?'

'I have to, there's no other option, but I can give you some wafers to eat'

'That's so kind of you, you're not like the rest of them.'

'I know, don't forget to flush the wrappers down the toilet.'

'Okay, bye,'

'Bye.'

Akshya locked the washroom again but left the lights on for Ahlam. Ahlam spent the rest of the nineteen hours in the washroom. He did everything he could to tick away the time there. He slept, talked to himself, and played games with himself, but nothing felt as amusing as acting his brains out. He even started craving a companion with whom he could chat, but neither a ghost nor a human accompanied him. Finally, Rohan opened the washroom door after 24 hours, and Ahlam's confinement ended.

**12**

As soon as Rohan opened the washroom door, a dehydrated Ahlam crawled out of the washroom.

'How was the experience,' said Rohan.

'Horrendous,'

'I think you have learned your lesson.'

'Yes I have, Rohan.'

'Don't you dare call me by my name.'

'What should I call you then?'

'Sir!'

'Okay sir,' said Ahlam, nodding

'Where would you like to sleep now?'

'On the floor, sir.

'Nice, find yourself a bedsheet and go to sleep.'

'Okay, sir, good night.'

Ahlam grabbed his bedsheet and slept like a baby.

The next day he got up and dressed himself for attending lectures. He left his room by 8:00 am sharp, and as Ahlam walked by the hallway, a person banged his shoulders into Ahlam's. It was Akshya.

'Hey, what's up?' Akshya said.

'Nothing much, what about you?' Ahlam said.

'Same here, boring day as usual.'

'No day is a boring day, you are just feeling lethargic, and that's why you're feeling it's a boring day.'

'You talk too much of philosophy!'

'No, I do not.'

'What are you studying at St. Xavier's?'

'Mass media, what about you?'

'Economics.'

'Oh, you're into mathematics and stuff?'

'No, but my dad is.'

'Cool, so you're heading towards your class?'

'Yeah, I can accompany you to your class, if you're okay with it.'

'Yeah, sure.'

Ahlam and Akshya appeared to build a friendly bond even though Akshya was a bully, and he bullied Ahlam on the first day of college. Akshya was distinct from his friends. *No one is born a thief; likewise, no one is born a bully.* Bullies are people who are bullied by other people. Akshya became a bully because he always felt he was powerless, weak, and insecure, and he only felt stronger by making other people feel even smaller than he did. Akshya was bullied during his school days as he was obese and academically weak and he felt severely depressed and suicidal as a kid. He started feeling heartbroken when he became a bully himself because he thought once he would become a bully, no one would bully, attack, or badmouth him. But it only got worse, it only gave a chance to those whom he bullied to criticise and judge him. He felt like he was absolutely nothing. He was only drowning in despair. Then, he decided he will disguise himself as a bully but will never actually bully people, instead, he will help those people.

Ahlam attended the first lecture at his college. It was somewhat okay, the professor was good, and the crowd seemed cool, but Ahlam wasn't able to befriend anybody. Everyone seemed uninterested in any kind of interaction. As Ahlam was walking out of the classroom, a poster on the wall caught his eye.

*NOTICE: AUDITIONS FOR THE ST. XAVIER'S DRAMA CLUB Auditions for the St. Xavier's Drama Club will be held on Monday, September 10. Below are the details.*

*Date: September 10, 2006*

*Venue: Auditorium*

*Classes: Freshers*

*Categories: acting*

*Interested Students will select one of the scenes to enact. They are expected to memorize the same for the audition. Please note that the students will not be allowed to read from the paper.*

1. *Atticus Finch's closing argument in 'To Kill a Mocking Bird'*

2. *Chaplin's last speech from 'The Great Dictator'*

Ahlam got exhilarated and scraped the poster off the wall and hid it inside his bag.

13

A hlam entered his hostel room without making any noise.

'Look, our little thief is here.' Rohan said.

'Mind your language; I'm not a thief!' Ahlam said.

'Prove it.'

'How?'

'Show us your bag.'

'No, it's my stuff.'

As Ahlam was busy arguing with Rohan, another bully came and grabbed Ahlam's legs and pulled them, causing Ahlam to fall on his face. Rohan snatched the bag from Ahlam and took out the poster.

'*Auditions for the St. Xavier's Drama Club*' Rohan read the poster loudly.

'Give it back to me.' Ahlam said.

'This little kid wants to audition for the drama club, which scene are you going to enact? Ahlam's closing argument in *Please Don't Beat Me Up* or Ahlam's last speech from *Beaten to Death by Bullies*.'

'Leave me alone, I didn't steal it, I took it off the wall for a private purpose.'

'You have stolen it, you filthy liar, keep yourself and your insipid dreams out of this room.'

Ahlam ran out of the room, with his bag wide open, and sat on one of the seats in the auditorium.

'Ahlam!' Someone shouted.

Ahlam turned his head and saw Akshya walking down the auditorium stairs.

'Are you really going to audition?'Akshya said.

'Yes, I am.'Ahlam said.

'I'm going to audition too.'

'Are you a cinema freak just like me?'

'I am! I am an aspiring actor.'

'Finally, I found my person, I'm an aspiring actor too.'

'Let's prepare for this audition together.'

'Why not?'

Ahlam and Akshya prepared for the audition together. Ahlam chose to enact the scene from 'To Kill a Mocking Bird' and Akshya chose to enact the scene from 'The Great Dictator'.

When Ahlam stood on the stage to perform, the bullies came out of nowhere and started hooting.

'Go on, perform the scene, oh wait! From where did you receive the information about this audition? From the poster that you stole from the school lobby?' Shouted Rohan while sitting in the middle of the auditorium. Ahlam kept standing on the stage with a gloomy face. Everyone was looking at him, and he felt nervous. He wanted to act but wasn't able to, so, he picked up his bag and left the stage.

It was Akshya's turn now. Akshya felt frightened because if his friends find out that Ahlam and he planned to participate in this audition together, they will treat him the same way they treat Ahlam, and he will have to go through all the things that he went through while he was in school. So he left backstage thereafter and followed Ahlam into the room.

'Why did you leave the stage?› Akshya said.

'Because I can't stand these people, I came here because I thought I would get the opportunity to perform in front of thousands of people, but this is not an opportunity; this is adversity.› Ahlam said.

'Ahlam, it feels awful when people don't leave a single event to criticise us, but we have to face these people and keep growing, stand up on that stage, and show the people what you have prepared.'

'What if they kept hooting?'

'*Ignorance is bliss.*'

'Okay, I'll perform and shut these people up.'

Ahlam went to the auditorium again. He gathered up all his courage and began to perform. As soon as words came out of Ahlam's mouth, the whole stadium went silent. It wasn't looking like it was Ahlam Siddique performing, it looked like it was Atticus Finch delivering the closing argument. His acting was surreal. Everyone's jaws dropped, and their eyes became wide. The bullies who were hooting couldn't believe it was Ahlam performing, the boy they bullied every day for their pleasure. Ahlam ended his act with the dialogue.

*Now I am confident that you gentlemen will review without passion the evidence that you have heard, come to a decision, and restore this man to his family.*

*In the name of God, do your duty. In the name of God, believe Tom Robinson.*

Everyone gave Ahlam a standing ovation, even the bullies couldn't resist themselves. The bullies realised that the boy they bullied every day looks cowardly from the outside but upholds a great talent inside that nobody in this college does. They never bullied Ahalm again, and they started behaving politely with him.

**14**

Ahlam and Akshya both got into the drama club of St. Xavier's and were declared the head of the drama club. They performed various acts and plays throughout their college lives and formed an inseparable bond. From playing the roles of Ennis and Jack in an adaptation of Brokeback Mountain to playing the roles of Stoney and Link in Encino Man's adaptation. They took the whole college by storm with their acting skills. Not even a single seat went unoccupied when they used to perform. People used to climb up the balconies of the auditorium to watch them perform. Acting wasn't the only thing they were good at, they were also academically bright students. They maintained their GPAs above 3.5 and came out as college toppers in their respective courses.

Ahlam and Akshya both wanted to become established actors in the Movieland. Both of them saw the same dream, both manifested the same dream, and both waited twenty-one years to transform their dream into reality.

The dream they invested their lives into seemed insipid until Slumdog Millionaire won the Academy Award for Best Picture. Slumdog Millionaire was the first American film ever that was entirely shot in India and starred an ensemble Indian cast. When Slumdog Millionaire took the Oscars by storm in 2008, it opened the gates for those Indian kids who grew up with a dream of standing on the stage in Dolby Theatres with a golden statue in their hands. Their false hopes converted into hopes when they saw Dev Patel being recognised by the Oscars.

Ahlam and Akshya just needed to make their way through those doors and enter into a reality dreamt by millions. They decided they would live their dream together.

To live their dream life, they needed to jump over all the stumbling blocks. Their parents' approval, acceptance into a prestigious American university in Los Angeles, and funds. It wasn't an easy task to do. Ahlam knew his abba would never pay a penny for his education in America. His abba hated those people who left the countries they were born in and got themselves settled in a foreign land. His abba considered those people anti-nationalists.

Ahlam had to tell his abba that he wants to study in America. So, one day he decided to visit his Abba for negotiations.

*knock knock*

'Whose there?' Abba said.

'It's me Abba.' Ahlam said.

'Who?'

'Are you kidding me? I just referred to you as Abba, how many kids do you have?'

'Just one blockhead kid.'

'Okay, that's me, by the way.'

'Oh, it's you, Ahlam!'

Ahlam's abba opened the gate with a broad smile.

'You don't remember my voice anymore?'

'I do, you know, I am getting older day by day, so it's hard sometimes to remember things.'

'Isn't it a symptom of Alzheimer's?'

'What the hell is Alzheimer's?'

'When you start forgetting everything as each day passes by, it›s called Alzheimer's.'

'Neither have I heard of this disease, nor do I have it.'

'Abba, stop being so careless about your health and visit a doctor as soon as possible.'

'No, I won't, Now stop being my dad and tell me what's going on in your life?'

'Nothing much, your son came out as a topper of his college.'

Abba jumped out of his skin as he couldn't believe his dumb Ahlam, who once failed in sixth grade, had topped his college.

'I'm so proud of you, Ahlam; I really can't believe my ears. Just keep working hard and make us prouder.'

'I will abba.'

'Now that you have completed your college with distinction, you should visit my office on Monday.'

'Why Abba?'

'For a job.'

'For a job?'

'Yes, I'll talk to my boss and will have you in my company as an employee.'

'But I don't want to work in your company.'

'Why?'

'Because I hate the concept of a 9-to-5 job, and I'd rather die than indulge myself in a regular, wearisome job.'

'If this is what you believe, then I should kill myself too because I'm also doing a regular, wearisome 9-to-5 job'

'Abba we all have different notions, you can stand working a 9-to-5 job, but I can't.'

'What do you want to do then?'

'I want to go to America.'

'For what?'

'To pursue a master's degree in journalism.'

'So, you want to show your back to the country that you grew up in, and want to run to a foreign land.'

'Abba, don't get started now.'

'Run away if you want to, but don't show me your face ever again.'

'Abba, I'm not running away from my country, I'll be back as soon as I complete my degree.'

'India doesn't give out master's degrees anymore?'

'Abba, I have lived in India my whole life, and now I want to experience a different culture.'

'Do whatever you want to do, but I won't pay a penny for this loathsome act.'

'I didn't even ask you for money; I just needed a little support from you.'

'I don't support anti-nationalists.'

Ahlam had it enough, he went to his room, collected his belongings, stuffed them inside a bag, and left the house. Abba wanted to stop Ahlam, but his beliefs didn't let him. Ahlam gave a ring to Akshya and told him to meet him at the college campus.

**15**

Ahlam and Akshya met each other at Xavier's campus.

'My abba didn't agree to pay a penny for my further education.' Ahlam said.

'My father agreed in a snap, he was ecstatic when I told him that I want to do my master's in America.› Akshya said.

'Lucky Pal, what should I do now?'

'Apply for a loan.'

'For fifty-lakhs?'

'Yeah!'

'Immigration officers will reject my visa if I'll fund my entire master's on loan.'

'Then do something, we saw a dream together, we will live it together, I'm not leaving you behind.'

'I'll arrange the funds, don't worry!'

Ahlam knew what he had to do. His childhood friend Rahim, with whom he saw American Beauty, had inherited his abba's jewellery shop, and Ahlam heard from somewhere that he was operating at a profit.

The next day, he visited the *Noor Jewellery Shop*. He saw Rahim sitting on a big black chair at the payment counter. He advanced inside with a big smile on his face.

'As-Salaam-Alaikum, my old friend!' Ahlam said.

'As-Salaam-Alaikum, who are you?' Rahim said.

'You don't remember your childhood best friend?'

'Which one are you?'

'The one that made you watch American Beauty.'

'I knew I had seen this face before, but I couldn't remember where. How are you doing, Ahlam?'

'I'm doing great!'

'Good to hear. What made you visit me after four years?'

'I am in a bit of a problem, so I thought I would ask my childhood best friend for some help.'

'Oh, what happened?'

'Have you ever heard about UCLA?'

'It's a university in Los Angeles, isn't it?'

'Yes, University of California, Los Angeles.'

'What about it?'

'I got into it.'

'Congratulations Ahlam, You came a long way. Now I can sing that song, *America se aaya mera dost*, every time I'll meet you.'

'Your humour is still the same.'

'I know, so tell me what I can help you with?'

'You can help me with some money.'

'You want a loan?'

'I do.'

'How much?'

'Thirty-Lakhs'

'Thirty lakhs? This is sarcasm, right?'

'No, this is not, I really do want some money, and I couldn't think of any person other than you who could lend me such a big amount.'

'I don't think I can lend you thirty lakhs, if you had asked for ten lakhs, then I would never have denied it.'

'What about twenty lakhs?'

'Give me a moment to think.'

Rahim started turning the pages of his account diary, and as each page turned, the wrinkles on his forehead became more intense.

'Okay, I'll lend you twenty lakhs.'

'Thank you so much, Rahim, you have always been there for me, whenever or wherever I needed you, you are really my best friend indeed.'

'It's nothing, just return me the money as soon as you land yourself a job.'

'I will, I promise'

'Allah hafiz.'

'Allah hafiz.'

Ahlam was elated because he was able to arrange twenty lakhs. Now, there was nobody left whom he could have asked for a loan, *the perks of being a wallflower,* if you understand what I mean, the less you interact with people, the lesser people are there for you to help you.

Ahlam went to SBI and applied for a loan of thirty lakhs.

Everything was working well for Ahlam, he had everything in place. He had the acceptance letter from UCLA, and he had the funds ready but one thing was missing, the support of his parents and their acceptance of his dream.

But Ahlam was determined to show abba his power of manifestation, and he knew, one day, when he'll win an Oscar and make his country proud, his abba will be the one who'll open the gates of his house with a proud and broad smile.

**16**

Ahlam and Akshya packed their bags, arranged their visas and passports, and booked a flight to the Movieland, *Los Angeles*. They boarded their flight on December 20, 2009.

With a heart full of desires, two solivagants were on their way to their dream city. Their dreams felt like acatalepsy for others, whenever they tried to explain their dreams to other people, they couldn't comprehend it.

'People say, as soon as you land in Los Angeles, you can feel the presence of movies there.' Akshya said.

'How?' Ahlam said, with curiosity.

'All you'll perceive is people moving around in fancy clothing, glamorous shoes, sparkly eyes, curly hair just like the 80s, and milk-like skin.'

'Americans are extremely fair-skinned, aren't they?'

'Indeed, they got it from their ancestors.'

'They look like, they never got out of their house, and didn't let a beam of sunlight touch them ever.' Ahlam said, jokingly.

'Yeah, blue eyes, fair skin, and beautiful faces, they have it all, What do we have?'

'*Hamare pass Maa hai!*'

'Stop kidding Ahlam.'

'Alright, don't incur your wrath on me.'

'I'm not, I'm angry with my luck, all we have is brown skin, which our ancestors gave us as a stroke of bad luck.'

'Stop talking absurd, Akshay, we have to envy what we have, every person is built uniquely, and does it even matter if we have brown skin and they have white skin, all that matters is your talent, your art that you manifest, and the dreams you see.'

'It's all philosophy, Ahlam, as soon as you land in America, you will face the harsh reality.'

'Rely upon your talent, not on luck.'

'*You're talking about luck?* Wouldn't it be easier if we would have been born in America, not in India? All the lies we spoke, the unfaithfulness we showed to our parents, the amount of money we spent to come here, your living expenses, and all the suffering we're going to get through, we wouldn't have to do any of that if we would have been born fortuitous.'

'I know how you're feeling right now, and I know we came a long way, we suffered, and we worked hard, but I'm telling you it's going to be worth it in the end, and in the end, you're going to come to me and whisper in my ears, you were right!'

'But what if Hollywood fails us? Do we have any backup?'

Hearing this, Ahlam went into a deep thought state, he started thinking about his decision of being an actor again and he took a moment to reflect.

*What if this is a pipe dream? and I manifested something that might never come true. If Akshya's anticipation turns into a reality. I would lose everything I have, and I would never get back the things that I already lost.*

*My ammi, my abbu, my home, and everything that I ever envied would fade away in a snap of time, I'm like a fish that tried to swim in an ocean full of other hungry fishes, they all wanted food, but the lucky ones gets it and the rest of them dies out of hunger, just like that many aspiring actors come to Hollywood with a heart full of desires, but the lucky ones gets through and the rest of them annihilate into the air.'*

'Should I go back to where I came from and start from scratch or continue on this journey and face the consequences.' Ahlam mumbled loudly.

'You want to go back where you came from?' Akshya said.

'I don't want to, but what if we came here only to dig our own graves.'

'What do you mean?'

'What if we don't end up becoming actors and end up as labourers or workers just like other aspiring actors, if that happens, I will kill myself for sure.'

'We both will, but what is the harm in trying once, *why don't we try living our life before killing ourselves?*

'Alright, we saw a dream, and we will live it to the fullest.'

Air India flight B-747 arrived at Los Angeles International Airport. Ahlam and Akshya got off the plane and picked up their baggage, and as soon as they stepped out of the airport's exit. Their jaws dropped, and they were left gobsmacked.

It felt like they were watching their dream world with open eyes.

**17**

Ahlam and Akshya could see the Hollywood sign, it was there, up on the hills, far away.

'This is splendid, I can't believe I'm seeing something that I have always seen in photos and movies.' Ahlam said.

'I know, after seeing this, I feel, this is the Movieland, and now we're are the Movielanders.' Akshya said.

'I have seen pictures of many actors with this sign in the background.'

'Yeah, I have seen a picture of Marilyn Monroe with this hill in the background.'

'I can feel my dream coming true now, let's click our pictures with this sign in the background.'

They both got their pictures clicked in front of Hollywood Hill, and then they stuffed their bags into a taxi and went rolling down the Hollywood boulevard. They couldn't get their eyes off the Hollywood Walk of Fame and the authentic Hollywood they saw only in movies.

*I can see my name on the Hollywood Walk of Fame, among all the stars, there will lie a star down there with the name Ahlam Siddique on it.*

*This is the place where movies are made, this is the place where dreams are either turned into reality or just left with the title 'A dream that never came true'. This exquisite place is going to be my new home, and these people are going to be my people, I don't care if the world comes crashing down; I would never give up on my dreams now.* Ahlam said to himself.

Ahlam and Akshya got out of the taxi and went to take a stroll in Beverly Hills.

'This is the place where most of the celebrities reside, from Jennifer Aniston to Madonna, everyone lives here.' Ahlam said.

'And one day we will live here too.' Akshya said.

'We will, but for now, we have to look for a home closer to Hollywood and UCLA.'

'But houses here will cost us a lifetime, we cannot afford to live near Hollywood.'

'Then, what should we do?'

'We can live in Downtown; it would cost around fifty bucks a month.'

'How could we? Downtown is a place for homeless people, and crime is so prevalent in that area.'

'If we live in a posh area, then we will be out of money soon, and then we have to work jobs, you want to do that?'

'What's the problem with working jobs? Some extra cash wouldn't harm us!'

'We can't study and work simultaneously; it is impossible.'

'It's not impossible, we will manage.'

'How?'

'We will attend lectures at UCLA until 2:00 pm, and then we will spend the rest of the day auditioning, and at night we will work jobs.'

'We'll be exhausted.'

'We have to lose something to gain something, you know, *the balance of life.*'

'But we can't work in America, we are here on a student visa, and international students in America can't work jobs off campus.'

'Then we'll find ourselves jobs on campus, it'll be much easier.'

'It won't be easier, there are fewer jobs for Indians and more jobs for Americans, and somehow if we land a job, we can't work more than twenty hours a week.'

'Twenty hours a week?'

'Yes!'

'That would bring a very small amount of money.'

'Exactly,'

'Leave it, we'll think about it later.'

Ahlam and Akshya decided to visit Downtown to look for a home, and as soon as their feet were ascending towards Downtown, a grotesque view unfolded in front of their eyes. and they couldn't believe what they were seeing there.

**18**

Ahlam and Akshya saw countless homeless people on the streets, living in a queue in houses made of wood and polythene. It melted Ahlam's heart. Even though he's from Mumbai and has seen numerous people living on the streets and in slums but Downtown's state is much worse. He expected life in Los Angeles to be lavish and joyful, but it wasn't even close to that. The police were behaving rudely with the homeless, and people were brawling over small things.

Ahlam and Akshya were strolling Downtown, and all of a sudden Ahlam heard a voice. It was a woman screaming for help. A man dressed in black was snatching a woman's bag, but no one was willing to help. Ahlam ran and pushed the man, making him fall hard on the floor. The thief stood up and kicked Ahlam in the stomach. Ahlam crouched and screamed as loud as he could. He was in immense pain. Akshya held Ahlam up and took him to the L.A. Downtown Medical Centre. The woman that Ahlam helped went with them.

The doctor examined Ahlam, and reports came out normal, but Ahlam was advised to stay in the hospital for a night. Akshya needed to find an apartment for both of them to live in, so he left the hospital immediately after seeing the reports.

The woman that Ahlam helped, took the initiative to stay with Ahlam in the hospital to show some gratitude.

'What is your name?' Ahlam said

'Rubina,' she said.

'Are you an Indian?'

'No, I'm from Pakistan.'

'Where in Pakistan?'

'Peshawar, where are you from?'

'Mumbai, India'

'It is a great feeling when you see someone familiar, isn't it?'

'Indeed, it is!'

'By the way, I'm grateful for what you have done for me today, I will never forget about it.'

'It was nothing, don't be lame.'

'It was everything to me, that bag that you saved from the thief, contained my passport.'

'Really?'

'Yes,'

'What do you do in Los Angeles?'

'I work in adult films.'

'Are you a porn star?'

'Yes, I am!'

'It was your dream to work in porn movies?'

'No, it wasn't, I was an aspiring actress, but my luck turned away as soon as I came to Los Angeles.'

'What happened? Tell me everything.'

'I was born and brought up in Peshawar, my abba was a cobbler and my ammi was a tailor, I grew up in a house made of mud with my five siblings, life was good until I started daydreaming, I wanted to become an actress but I knew my abba would kill me if I utter a word about my dream, honour killing is like a tradition in Pakistan, so I ran away from my country and came to Los Angeles but everything didn't go as I expected it to be, I ended up getting no roles here and I was out of money soon but then one day, a director approached me with a movie offer, I agreed to it and signed the agreement but I later found out, it was an offer for a porn movie and I was stuck with it and if I could have refrained from doing it, he could have taken legal actions against me so, I did the movie, I despised myself for doing it but I wanted some money so, I got involved in this industry so much that I couldn't get out of it.'

'I'm sorry for what you have been through.'

'Don't be, I accepted my life, and I'm not sorry about it anymore, my tears are dried up already.'

The story that Rubina told Ahlam made him feel so pity for her that tears started rolling out of his eyes. Ahlam felt an overwhelming feeling, as what will happen if he'd end up like Rubina. His train of thought was moving, but Rubina ceased its engine and insisted Ahlam to go for a walk outside if he was feeling okay. Ahlam agreed, and they went for a walk.

# 19

Ahlam and Rubina met five hours ago due to an accident, but now it seems like they have known each other for a long time.

They shared everything with each other while walking together. It was a starry night, and people were having sleepless nights at their homes. Rubina was liking Ahlam's company, and Ahlam was liking Rubina's company.

Soon, Ahlam got tired and sat on a bench. He felt someone's hand on his shoulder. It was Akshya's. He was able to find an affordable room for himself and Ahlam. They spent the rest of the night in the hospital, and the very next day, they went to see the house.

It wasn't a house, it was a small room with a kitchen, toilet, and washroom in it.

'You found a room only for yourself?' Ahlam said.

'This is for both of us.' Akshya said.

'But you were telling me, you found a house to live in.'

'This is what people consider a house in America.'

'This is only a room, Akshya.'

'This is all we can afford.'

'We can't live here, there's no space for anything, how could you fit two beds in this small room?'

'We have to share a bed.'

'This is what the American Dream looks like?'

'I suppose it is!'

'This is bigger than mine.' Rubina said.

Ahlam, Akshya, and Rubina giggled, and soon their giggles turned into laughter. Ahlam and Akshya accepted their fate and shifted into the house the very next day, and they were accompanied by Rubina in shifting.

The day passed without any adversity, but they didn't know that their lives were about to take a turn and that every day from now on would be filled with lots of struggle. It was the silence before the storm.

**20**

Ahlam woke up the next day and dressed in his best attire. A white Polo T-shirt, a caramel-brown overcoat with caramel-brown trousers, black sneakers, and wavy hair with a string of hairs hanging between his forehead. He was carrying the whole 90s with him. He wore wired headphones, played 'Everybody Wants to Rule the World' and walked down Hollywood Boulevard, tickling his feet all over the Hollywood Walk of Fame. He reached UCLA and advanced into the university with his *main character's energy*. Everyone was looking at Ahlam with creases on their foreheads. Ahlam was thinking, he was slaying among all the other college students, but that wasn't the cause. Everybody was looking at him because they were seeing a brown boy dressed like a movie star, walking confidently through the hallway. 9/11 happened nine years ago, but its impact was still prevailing, and it still made people watch people of different ethnicities with ferocity.

He walked inside the classroom and sat on the sixth seat in the tenth row. Everyone was avoiding sitting near him, and as soon as Ahlam realised that, his main character's energy faded away and he started thinking.

*Why am I here? Everyone is looking at me like I'm Osama Bin Laden, is this how they are going to behave with me every day? I wish someone would come and sit with me because I'm feeling like an imposter among all these people.*

No one took the initiative to sit with Ahlam, and he felt awkward all day, which made him feel extremely agitated.

Ahlam departed from the college at 2:00 p.m., and now it was time for him to audition for movies. He went to Hollywood by taxi, got freshened up, and began looking for auditions. He saw a flyer for a short film, named 'The New Tenants'. A male aged between 20 and 30, a very leading man, handsome, and physically fit, was required for the role. As soon as he saw the flyer, he went to audition for that short film.

He entered a small room and saw an ample number of people standing in a queue. Those people had everything, they were handsome, charming, and had bodies like supermodels. Ahlam didn't even stand a chance against those men, but still, he gave it a shot. He saw many people leaving the room with dejection on their faces. Ahlam knew what was going to happen next.

'Next,' the casting director said, aloud.

'Hi!' Ahlam said.

'What's your name?'

'Ahlam Siddique.'

'Ethnicity?'

'South Asian,'

'Pakistani?'

'No, Indian.'

'So, you're a brown-skinned Indian and a Muslim?'

'Yes, I am, do you have any problem with that?'

'The whole of America has a problem with people like you, you filthy people killed our people, and now you have the audacity to come to our country and compete with our people to find yourself work, shame on you!'

'Did I kill your people?'

'Yes, you did.'

'I wish you had a brain! People like us didn't kill your people, people called terrorists killed your people.'

'You believe that?'

'I do, and every Muslim is not a terrorist.'

'Are you done with your patriotism?'

'Yes, I am, I could continue arguing with you, *but you either keep hitting the wall until you bleed or you just hit your head once and get away from it to save yourself from bleeding,* and I opt for option number two.'

'Do you have anything else to tell us or show us?'

'Yes, I have; can I have the script?'

'There's no script; just read a monologue from any movie.'

Ahlam recalled the time when he played Atticus Finch in St. Xavier's drama club's audition. Ahlam started performing Atticus Finch's closing argument in *To Kill a Mockingbird,* but the casting director stopped him when he was about to speak the third dialogue and asked him to leave. Ahlam got infuriated, punched the wall right behind him, and left the room. It was the first day when Ahlam faced the harsh reality of Hollywood and got to know about the fate of outsiders in the industry.

# 21

Ahlam returned home to Akshya, who was sick due to hay fever.

'How did the first day go?' Akshya said.

'It went great, people were super friendly to me, and everyone loved me.' Ahlam said.

'Really?'

'No, everybody hated me.'

'What happened?'

'This world is full of racist people who discriminate against you because you're a Muslim or a brown-skinned person.'

'I told you that already, you either face the reality or you don't face it at all.'

'I realised it now, I went for an audition.'

'How did it go?'

'I was performing Atticus Finch's closing argument just like I did in Xavier›s, and the casting director stopped me in between and asked me to leave.'

'I told you, these people don't envy us because we don't lick their feet.'

'Hollywood is the worst place for aspiring actors, the only thing you get in return is your shattered dream.'

'But we'll never stop auditioning, God's watching us. The more we work hard, the closer we advance to our dream. My mother used to say that *if nothing's happening, then it's an indication that something's going to happen.*'

'So, God is just testing our patience?'

'Exactly, now calm down and doze off for some hours.'

Ahlam felt relaxed talking to Akshya, he laid down next to Akshya, placing his fretting thoughts aside, and dozed off for five hours.

# 22

Ahlam woke up after five hours, and it was 8:00 am in the morning.

'Aren't we running late for college?' Ahlam said.

Akshya woke up and looked at the clock.

'We're running one hour late, actually.' Akshya said.

Akshya and Ahlam went hysterical in that small room and started running here and there. Both dry-cleaned themselves and went to college.

As soon as they entered the classroom, everybody looked at them like deer have entered a lion's cave. The day went similarly to yesterday, and this starring game never ended.

They faced racism at UCLA every day. The racism tendencies went so extreme that once a group of boys pulled a Sikh boy's turban and bullied him for half an hour.

In America, people just watch and make videos of people who are facing atrocities, but no one comes across to help the person in need, even if the person is crying for help. If you'll be dying on a street full of hundreds of people, not one person will call 911. America looks captivating only in your imagination, but when you see reality with your eyes, you will disdain yourself because you'll find out that your imaginary city isn't quite as intriguing as you suppose it to be, it's the opposite of that. In the 1950s, black people weren't even allowed to live in certain neighbourhoods. The property papers used to mention that no person of negro blood could own the property. But black people tried to make their way and faced severe challenges.

Does our skin colour and ethnicity define us? Can you tell by guessing someone's ethnicity, if they are terrorists or normal people? Can you fathom someone's personality just by their ethnicity? No, you can't. But people have made their own parameters of understanding and invented their own terminologies.

Ahlam knew if he wanted to become an actor, he had to rise above all the racial and colour discrimination; otherwise, Hollywood would become nothing but an ordinary city for him, just like Mumbai.

Ahalm and Akshya used to go to auditions every day, but they used to hear the same words every day.

*'We don't find you suitable for this role, or we needed a man of Caucasian race as our lead actor, not an ethnically ambiguous man, or you don't fit perfectly for the role, or you're not a good actor.› This continued for three years.*

Ahlam and Akshya didn't find a single role in three years, their master's was about to be over, and they spent most of the time auditioning and didn't give a thought to the university or a job. Their GPAs went down. They didn't find themselves any sort of internship because they either could have studied hard and found themselves a job or could have stayed on their path to Dreamworld and made their dream come true. They chose the path to their Dreamworld because they were in the movieland and they had already declared themselves as movielanders and movielanders are stubborn, they don't deflect from their paths. When they were busy transforming their dreams into reality, they lost the opportunity to seek jobs.

Ahlam and Akshya were in America on a student visa, and they were about to be provided with a work visa for three years. If they didn't find themselves a job and didn't get sponsored in the next three years, there could be a probability that they would have to return to their home country.

Ahlam and Akshya never turned their backs on their dream and faced the risk of deportation back to their country with fortitude. They kept auditioning for another year. They used to sit outside the audition room for consecutive nights, they used to sleep in the queue; they ate roadside food; and the auditioning never went without begging for roles, but the casting directors were stubborn; no amount of begging would ever have convinced them. They did everything just to face the rejection.

**23**

It's been four long years, and Akshya was exhausted. He used to cry every day in the corner of his room, and soon he started to have hallucinations. He started telling people that he could see ghosts, and everyone thought he was going crazy. Ahlam used to take care of him all the time, spending less time auditioning. Ahlam used to take him to the hospital, and every doctor told him that he was schizophrenic and suffering from terminal cancer simultaneously.

Ahlam knew Akshya's dreams had already shattered, but he refrained from telling Akshya. Cancer made Akshya's life so miserable, that he started to lose control over his body. He used to puke blood, excrete on the bed, and break things all around the room. He stopped eating, which made him very thin, and his ribs were clearly visible through his skin.

People say Los Angeles is a city where dreams come true, but for Akshya, the city turned out to be the worst destination he could ever reach, even worse than hell. In every third house in Los Angeles, there lies a shattered dream and people hanging on the ceiling.

Akshya tried killing himself several times. On one occasion, he tried to jump in front of a moving taxi, but the taxi driver pulled the brake. On another occasion, he went to a medical store and bought different medicines, crushed all of them to a powdered form with a mortar and pestle, dissolved it in a bottle of beer, and drank it, and as soon as he drank it, he puked all over the floor and fainted. Doctors saved his life and advised Ahlam to send Akshya to a mental asylum.

Ahlam wanted to cure Akshya but didn't know how. He tried several things to make him feel better, but nothing seemed to work out. Ahlam told Rubina everything, and Rubina came up with a plan.

Rubina advised taking Akshya on a road trip to Hollywood Hill to remind him that he didn't come to this city to live a life full of misery, he came here for a dream. A dream he›s seen since he was seven years old, and if he didn't stand on his feet now, he never could again.

They got dressed up in simple summer shirts and cozy shorts and stuffed their bags into the car's trunk. Ahlam took his Ford Thunderbird out of his garage. Ahlam sat in the driver's seat, Akshya sat in the front passenger seat, and Rubina sat in the backseat, and they drove to Hollywood Hill.

They started rolling up Mulholland Drive in their open car. With their hands up in the air, the wind touching their faces, and their hair floating in the air, *Lay All Your Love on Me* by ABBA was playing on the stereo. Rubina stood up and started shouting the lyrics.

*Don't go wasting your emotion*

*Lay all your love on me*

*Don't go sharing your emotion*

*Lay all your love on me*

The feeling was astounding and irreplaceable. As they were going up the road, Akshya's expression could tell that he was enjoying every bit of that moment. After two long years, Akshya was giggling like a baby and it felt like an overwhelming feeling to Ahlam to see his friend happy after years.

They reached the Hollywood Hill and went close to the Hollywood sign, and spent all the night just below it. Ahlam's dad jokes, stargazing, and the calmness of night made them feel like it was their leisure time, and they are still teenagers. *They were so close to reality, yet so far from their dreams.*

At dawn, they packed their bags and returned to their car so, the security wouldn't catch them. They all jumped into the car, and Ahlam started the engine. They were on their way down the Mulholland Drive when suddenly Akshya whispered something.

'Did you say anything?' Ahlam said.

'Yes,' Akshya said.

'What?'

'Take me to LAX.›

'LAX? The airport?'

'Yes,'

'But why?'

'I'll tell you later.'

Ahlam drove Akshya to LAX, and they got out of the car. Akshya held Ahlam's hand, and Ahlam doesn't seem to understand what is happening. But as soon as Ahlam looked at Akshya's hand, he saw his passport clenched in his fist, and then he saw Akshya's face and realised that tears were rolling down his face.

'What's happening, Akshya?' Ahlam said.

'I'm going back to India.' Akshya said.

'What? Why?'

'This city wrecked me, Ahlam, I came here with aspirations, but all I received was a trauma for a lifetime, I tried so hard to cope with the adversities but later gave up because I felt there was no meaning to this life. You wake up, go to the university, face all sorts of bullying there, and then you try to audition for movies to come face to face to rejection only. The dream I saw wasn't a dream, it was a pipe dream, I knew it would never come true but I still kept trying, and after some time I felt no urge to audition for anything, I let my dream disappear, and I tried to live it again, but it was too late.'

'Why are you saying this?'

'Because this is the reality, Ahlam, have you ever wondered why I tried killing myself several times?'

'I wondered, I always wondered, but always ended up with the same answer that, maybe you are going through tough times or you are seeing your dreams getting crushed.'

'You remember the time when we told each other *that we'll kill ourselves if we don't end up as actors*, and when I realised I couldn't live my dream life and couldn't get back my real one, and I was stuck in between, killing myself felt like an urge to me.'

'But you lived your whole life because of this dream, you came so far for this dream, and now you want to go home and give up?'

'I wasn't destined to be an actor, my destiny wants to take me somewhere else, and I want to go along with it because if I lose myself now, I'll lose myself forever.'

'So, you're going home forever and you're never coming back?'

'You will bring me back, when I'll die, spread my ashes on the Hollywood Hill, I will rest there forever.'

'Don't say that.'

'It's a dying person's wish, you have to fulfil it.'

Akshya hugged Ahlam for the last time. It was their moment, and they shared it with each other in melancholy with tears in their eyes. Akshya proceeded for the check-in, but he turned back, and they gazed at each other for the very last time, and Akshya yelled, '*Go live my dream*'. It was the last time they ever saw each other; Akshya passed away after one month.

**24**

Ahlam lost his best companion and was left alone on this journey. He had miles to cover in a short span of time.

In a span of four years, Ahlam auditioned for 126 movies, 80 short films, 32 documentaries, and 212 advertisements, but he got rejected for each one of them. The Green Hornet, The Other Woman, Midnight in Paris, Wanderlust, Detention, Life of Pi, About Time, Carrie, and The Theory of Everything were among them.

Deep inside, Ahlam knew he was going to end up like Akshya and Rubina, but Ahlam didn't want to go back home, so he started looking for a job as soon as he got a work visa. He finally got hired by the New York Times. He started avoiding auditions and kept himself busy with work. The pay was less, but his expenses were touching the sky.

One year passed, and he reached heights in the company. He got sponsored by the company and received a green card. He started earning 50,000 dollars a year, and he was grateful for his life, but he always felt a part of him is missing. After getting the green card, he started auditioning for movies again, but he was still unable to remove the tag of rejection. He was making a lot of money, but he was still staying in that one-room apartment in Downtown, Los Angeles. One day, Ahlam's ammi called him out of the blue and just asked one question: *'Are you the person now that you always wanted to be?'* After hearing this, he realised that he had left his dream far behind and had come so far to get himself stuck inside *the Circle of Life* that he always condemned. He stood still and reflected.

*I never wanted to work a 9-to-5 job, I condemned this way of living, but now I'm stuck with this lifestyle.*

Ahlam encouraged himself again, listened to his heart, and started spending most of his time auditioning. He got so involved in transforming his dream into a reality, that he left his job, and soon, all the money he had saved started disappearing.

Now, all he had was a dream and a house with unpaid rent. He used to spend all his time auditioning and sometimes didn't even return home.

One day, he came back home and saw all his stuff lying outside on the pavement. His landlord had kicked him out of the house due to unpaid rent. He had no place to live now, he left all his stuff there and started walking on the pavement. As he was walking away, he recalled his old friend Rubina and went straight to her house to reside there until he found himself a place to live. As soon as he knocked on the door, a woman peeked through a small window.

'What do you want?› The woman said.

'Are you really Rubina?' Ahlam said.

'Who's Rubina?'

'The girl that lives here.'

'Oh! That girl, it was a shame what happened to her.'

'What happened to her?'

'It was a tragic event, that girl married an alcoholic, and she had a baby with him. He used to abuse her every day, and one day she decided to bring her suffering to an end, so she shot herself, her husband, and her baby with a shotgun.'

Ahlam was left aghast after hearing the words that came out of that woman's mouth. He couldn't digest the fact that he lost another friend. He was hearing about his friend Rubina, whom he met a year ago, and now she was no more.

*I have a cursed life, whoever comes close to me, suffers something tragic, we all came here because of a dream but our fate was written with blood.* Ahlam mumbled.

# 25

Ahlam was devastated, and he questioned everything at that moment, His world seemed to collapse. He sat on the pavement along the road and started crying his heart out.

*Why me, why always me? Haven't I been through enough, Everything I do, turns into something miserable, I came here for this insipid dream of mine, but now I realise I should never have relied on it. I lost my parents, my friends, and every person I ever knew. This is life? If this life I don't want to live it anymore. I hate myself.*

Ahlam was crying heavily and shouting, and that is when he felt a tap on his shoulder. It was a woman dressed in a very sophisticated manner.

'Hi,' the woman said.

'I know what you're going to say now, you will tell me that I should stop shouting because it is bothersome, but I will shout as loud as I can, and I won't stop until my heart tells me to.' Ahlam shouted.

'No, you can shout, I have no problem with your venting.'

'Then, what do you want?'

'I was witnessing you from the nearby shop, and I feel you should visit my studio tomorrow.'

'I'm sorry! Who are you?'

'I'm a casting director, and I have cast several newcomers in many prominent movies.'

'Can I have your name?'

'Shirley Rich.'

'Shirley Rich?'

'Yeah,'

'You're the one that cast prominent actors in *Fiddler on the Roof, Cabaret,* and *Three Days of the Condor,* I can't believe you're inviting me to your studio. It's like I'm watching my dream come true.'

'I can understand how you're feeling right now, prepare yourself a monologue tomorrow'.

'How come, you want to me audition for you, you can cast anyone but why me?'

'I saw something in you, and I felt an urge to cast you in this movie I'm working for.'

Shirley Rich gave him her card and left, and as soon as she left, Ahlam started jumping up and down on the road, yelling, 'My life is about to change'.

**26**

Ahlam visited the studio the next day, situated on Hollywood Boulevard. He entered the room and saw Shirley Rich sitting there with a smile.

'Have you prepared any monologue?' Shirley Rich said.

'Yes, I did!' Ahlam said.

'Go on, show us what you have prepared.'

Ahlam stood in the spotlight and started performing.

*Son, we live in a world that has walls, and those walls have to be guarded by men with guns. Who's gonna do it? You? You, Lieutenant Weinberg? I have a greater responsibility than you can possibly fathom. You weep for Santiago, and you curse the Marines. You have that luxury. You have the luxury of not knowing what I know -- that Santiago's death, while tragic, probably saved lives; and my existence, while grotesque and incomprehensible to you, saves lives.*

Everybody realised it was the monologue by Jack Nicholson from A Few Good Men. Shirley Rich felt so powerful watching Ahlam perform the monologue, her jaw dropped, and she stood up and started clapping.

'Many people come and go, they always told me that they are inspired by me, and I just sit on this chair and smile, but today all I can say is, you inspired me Ahlam Siddique, and you're in for a ride. I'm casting you.' Shirley Rich said.

Ahlam's eyes gleamed, and his happiness was visible on his face, he stood there for a moment, because these kinds of moments might never come again. He silently went and shook Shirley Rich's hand, she provided him with details of the movie.

The movie was titled 'The Last Traveler'. Ingmar Bergman directed the movie, and Brittany Murphy was cast as his co-star. The script was about a man suffering from a terminal disease who decides to explore the world with his current girlfriend. Their lives were filled with ups and downs, but they still found a way to live it in the best way possible. Ahlam gave the performance of his lifetime. The movie was critically acclaimed and commercially successful. The Guardian called it the feel-good movie of the year with a five-star rating, and The Telegraph called it 'Sheer Perfection'.

On Thursday, January 14, the jury members announced the Academy Award nominations, and The Last Traveler became the most-nominated film of the year. Ahlam was nominated in the best actor category alongside Leonardo DiCaprio, Bryan Cranston, Matt

Damon, Michael Fassbender, and Eddie Redmayne. Brittany Murphy was nominated in the Best Actress category, Ingmar Bergman was nominated in the Best Director category, and the movie itself got nominated in the Best Picture, Best Original Screenplay, and Best Original Song categories.

# 27

Finally, it was the day that Ahlam dreamed about his whole life. The dream that helped him escape the adversities, the dream that made him the person that he is right now, and that dream is about to come true. It was the night of the Oscars. He got dressed in the same attire that he used to dream about. A black tuxedo with a white shirt, black shoes, a miniature bow tie, and goofy socks. Hairs combed to the right side.

He was surrounded by the paparazzi, and they were yelling Ahlam's name constantly. Ahlam was standing in the middle of the red carpet, and it felt impossible for him to digest all the stardom that he was receiving. He met many celebrities, and it was all praise for him. Ahlam was assigned a seat in the front row alongside Brittany Murphy. They both were giggling, chatting, and waiting restlessly for their respective categories. Robin Williams comes up on stage as the announcer to announce the Academy Award for best actor in a leading role, and his deep voice goes, 'The Academy Award for Best Actor in a Leading Role goes to Ahlam Siddique'. Ahlam bounces out of his chair in excitement, hugs Brittany Murphy, and walks up the stage, wiping his tears as commentators brief in the background.

*It is Ahlam Siddique's first Academy Award and as well as his first nomination. He is the first Indian actor to ever win an Academy Award.*

Robin Williams hands the Oscar to Ahlam, and he stands in front of thousands of people and gives his Oscar speech.

*'I am obliged that I received this prestigious award today. As artists, we manifest our art through our films and paintings, and we work so hard so we can earn just one thing as a reward for our manifestation and suffering, and today I got my reward in the form of this golden statue. This is the first trophy ever handed to me with my name on it. When I was in school, I never won any sort of prize there was, and I felt I wasn't worthy of anything, but today I feel I am worthy of something. All those children who saw a dream just like me but always wondered if it could ever come true, the doors are opened today; you just have to choose the right path. Last but not least, I love everything and everyone.'*

Ahlam looked down the stage and saw Heath Ledger, Philip Seymour Hoffman, Anna Nicole Smith, and Amy Winehouse cheering for him, and at that moment he felt pure eudaimonia.

*It was the night of the Oscars 2016 and Heath Ledger died in January 2008 as a result of an accidental overdose of medications.*

* 9 7 9 8 8 9 0 2 6 6 5 7 6 *